For my three treasures—Nicholas, Gavin, and Maggie
—J. P.

For Jen and our two little pirates, Emmett and Nate
— G. R.

A FEIWEL AND FRIENDS BOOK
An Imprint of Macmillan

A PIRATE'S GUIDE TO FIRST GRADE. Text copyright © 2010 by James Preller.
Illustrations copyright © 2010 by Greg Ruth. All rights reserved. Printed in September 2010
in the United States of America by Lehigh Phoenix, Rockaway, New Jersey.
For information, address Feiwel and Friends, 175 Fifth Avenue, New York, N.Y. 10010.

Library of Congress Cataloging-in-Publication Data Available

ISBN: 978-0-312-36928-6

Book design by Kathleen Breitenfeld
Feiwel and Friends logo designed by Filomena Tuosto

First Edition: 2010

The art was created with pencil, Sumi ink, watercolor oilstick, and pastels on paper.

10 9 8 7 6 5 4

www.feiwelandfriends.com

A Pirate's Guide

to First Grade

by

James Preller

illustrated by

Greg Ruth

FEIWEL AND FRIENDS

NEW YORK

 **Arrr!**

Shiver me timbers, what a slobberin' moist mornin'!

Me great scurvy dog slurped me kisser
when I was tryin' t' get me winks!

While I was wipin' the slime from me gob,

I remembered 'twas the first day of school.

I leaped out of bed . . .

shined me snappers,

and got dressed double quick.

Put on me hook, me boots,

me three-corner hat—

the only clothes fit for a pirate!

Down in the galley, I mashed me choppers on grub

and drowned it with grog. Time t' set sheets to the wind!

Me mother was soggy with fare-thee-wells,

fussing over this, that, and the other thing.

"Fair winds!" I exclaimed, and headed for me ship.

And a great, grand jolly boat it was!

"Ahoy, me hearties!" I cried. "Prepare to be boarded!"

Fore and aft bustled a salty crew of swabbies, sailing for adventure across the briny deep!

Strike up the band, me mateys, we'll sing a shanty.

"Fifteen men on a dead man's chest!"

"Land, ho!"

our lookout cried from the crow's nest.

We dropped anchor and smartly stepped forth
t' meet our new cap'n. Silver was her name,
and a fine old salt was she!

PATRICK
Elementa

Old Silver asked if I'd been t' school a'fore

and I replied,

"In truth, no nay ne'er!"

She said, "Then, you're in for a treat!"

I answered, "But it's swag I seek, and treasure!"

I stowed me gear and looked 'round,

a most wondrous sight filled me deadlights.

Cap'n Silver gathered us 'round for story time.

Blimey, it was a whale of a tale!

I'll make no bones about it, Cap'n Silver worked us like black dogs on a hot day. We counted and spelled 'till we nearly dropped, brain-addled and weary.

Mark me, I'd a rather trimmed the sails and polished brass

for all the achin' it gave me noggin.

When the bell clanged for recess, I scrambled straight

before me nose.

"Gangway, me hearties!"

Lads and lasses climbed and tumbled

'till we were all shipshape and seaworthy.

We even made one buccaneer walk the plank! Aye, fall in and it's shark bait ye be, then off to Fiddler's Green.

T'ward the end of day, I was feelin' ragged and
a wee bit downhearted.

Old Silver, she sized me up.

"Well, you seem as smart as paint to me.

Did ye not have a fine first day?"

"𝕬𝖗𝖗𝖗,"

I sighed. "'Twas good enough for lubbers, I suppose.

But where's me treasure?"

Old Silver, she frowned, then a light shined brightly in her goggles. "Aye, me bucko, I almost forgot...."

She handed me a map where $\mathbf{X}$ marked the spot.

I passed the mess and crossed the halls.

Until thar she blew—

me treasure!

Homework! A Pirate's Vocabulary

ADDLED
insane, or foolish

AFT
rear of ship

BUCCANEER
Caribbean pirate

CHOPPERS
teeth

CROW'S NEST
a platform near the top of the mast to give a lookout a better view

DEADLIGHTS
eyes

DOUBLE QUICK
in a hurry

FIDDLER'S GREEN
a pirate's idea of heaven

FORE
the bow or front of the ship

GALLEY
kitchen aboard a boat

GANGWAY
a warning to step aside

GOB
mouth

GOGGLES
eyes

GRUB
food